708

# Hanna Bear's Christmas

Text copyright © 2007 by Monica Devine

Illustrations copyright © 2007 by Sean Cassidy

Published in Canada by Fitzhenry & Whiteside,
195 Allstate Parkway, Markham, Ontario L3R 4T8

Published in the United States by Fitzhenry & Whiteside,
311 Washington Street, Brighton, Massachusetts 02135

www.fitzhenry.ca    godwit@fitzhenry.ca

10 9 8 7 6 5 4 3 2 1

**Library and Archives Canada Cataloguing in Publication**

Devine, Monica
Hanna Bear's Christmas / Monica Devine; illustrated by Sean Cassidy.

ISBN 978-1-55041-585-8

1. Bears—Juvenile fiction.  2. Christmas stories, American.
I. Cassidy, Sean, 1947-  II. Title.

PZ7.D48Ha 2007          j813'.54          C2006-906870-4

**U.S. Publisher Cataloging-in-Publication Data
(Library of Congress Standards)**

Devine, Monica.
Hanna Bear's Christmas / Monica Devine; illustrated by Sean Cassidy.
[32] p. :  col.  ill.; cm.
Summary: Hanna Bear wants to enjoy Christmas this year, but she will be asleep as usual. Her friends
promise to get Hanna up, but they must work together to stir the hibernating bear from her winter sleep.

ISBN-10: 1-55041-585-9    ISBN-13: 9781550415858
1. Christmas – Juvenile fiction.  2. Bears – Fiction—Juvenile literature.  I. Cassidy, Sean. II. Title.
[E] dc22  PZ7.D485  2007

Canada Council   Conseil des Arts
for the Arts      du Canada

ONTARIO ARTS COUNCIL
CONSEIL DES ARTS DE L'ONTARIO

Fitzhenry & Whiteside acknowledges with thanks the Canada Council for the Arts,
and the Ontario Arts Council for their support of our publishing program. We acknowledge
the financial support of the Government of Canada through the Book Publishing Industry
Development Program (BPIDP) for our publishing activities.

Design by Wycliffe Smith Design Inc.

Printed in Hong Kong

# Hanna Bear's Christmas

BY MONICA DEVINE

Illustrated by
Sean Cassidy

Fitzhenry & Whiteside

*For my sons, Zachary and Christopher*
  –Monica

*For Gail. Thanks for believing.*
  –Sean

One crisp fall evening, Hanna Bear sat on a hill eating fat,

juicy blueberries. A shimmering moon rose in the sky.

Hanna Bear looked up. She tipped her nose

and took a long, deep breath.

"Ah…," Hanna Bear said.

"I can smell the days

of winter coming."

The next day, Hanna Bear searched the forest until she discovered a fine, roomy den under the roots of an old spruce tree. On the floor of the den, she made a bed of grass, leaves, and moss. When she was finished, she gathered all her friends.

"It's time for me to go to sleep for the winter," Hanna Bear told them, "because *that* is what bears do." Her friends nodded.

"But this year, would you promise to wake me up for Christmas?" Hanna Bear asked.

"We've never done anything like that before," said the great bull moose.

"But we could," said the spruce grouse.

"After all, everyone deserves to see Christmas," the wise mountain goat added.

"Then it's settled. We'll have a merry Christmas!" Hanna Bear waved goodbye and crawled into her den.

While Hanna Bear slept, it snowed and snowed. Inside her warm den, Hanna Bear dreamed of hiking tall mountains and picking plump, juicy blueberries.

After many weeks, Christmas finally arrived.

"We mustn't forget to wake Hanna Bear," announced the wise mountain goat. All the animals gathered around the old spruce tree.

The mountain goat tipped his head and banged the tree with his horns.

*BAM, BAM, BAM!*

"Wake up for Christmas, Hanna Bear!" he cried. He butted the door with all his strength.

*BAM, BAM, BAM!*

But Hanna Bear did not stir.

"Your horns are too small," said the bull moose.

"I can wake her."

The moose dropped his mighty head and dragged his rack up and down the old spruce tree.

*CLICKETY, CLICKETY. CLACK, CLACK, CLACK!*

"Wake up for Christmas, Hanna Bear!" he cried.

He dragged his rack over and over again.

*CLICKETY, CLICKETY. CLACK, CLACK, CLACK!*

But Hanna Bear did not budge.

"Let me try," said the spruce grouse.

With a raucous flutter, he pumped his wings, flapping a thunderous sound.

*WHOMP, WHOMP. WHOMP, WHOMP, WHOMP!*

"Wake up for Christmas, Hanna Bear!" he cried. He flapped until his wings were all worn out.

*WHOMP, WHOMP. WHOMP, WHOMP, WHOMP!*

But Hanna Bear did not move.

"You simply weren't flapping fast enough," said the snowshoe hare. "I bet I can wake her."

She hopped onto the den and drummed steadily with her feet.

*THUMP, THUMP. THUMPETY, THUMP!*

"Wake up for Christmas, Hanna Bear," she shouted. She drummed faster and faster with all her might.

*THUMP, THUMP. THUMPETY, THUMP!*

But Hanna Bear would not wake up.

"Each one of us alone just isn't loud enough," said the wise mountain goat.

For a moment, the forest was silent.

Then—

*BAM, BAM, BAM!*

*CLICKETY, CLICKETY. CLACK, CLACK, CLACK!*

*WHOMP, WHOMP. WHOMP, WHOMP, WHOMP!*

*THUMP, THUMP. THUMPETY, THUMP!*

Together they butted, and scraped, and flapped, and
thumped so loudly that finally, FINALLY, Hanna Bear
poked her head out, rubbed her sleepy eyes, and said,
"What's all the ruckus?"

"MERRY CHRISTMAS, HANNA BEAR!"

Hanna Bear stepped out of her den. She had never seen snow so deep and bright. Spruce trees stood tall and quiet with snow glistening on their branches. Hanna Bear could see her breath. She sniffed the air—fresh and cold and wonderful.

But that wasn't all.

"Follow us," said the wise mountain goat.

The snow swished as they walked through the forest.

Moments later, they stopped.

"Look!" Hanna Bear cried.

"Oh my!" said Hanna Bear.

"Thank you for waking me for Christmas."

Soon a big, silver moon rose in the sky. Hanna Bear yawned. She took one last look at the cabin all aglow. The fresh, deep snow sparkled in the moonlight.

Together her friends led Hanna back to the den.

"This spring I'll wake up all by myself," she said.

"Because *that* is what bears do."